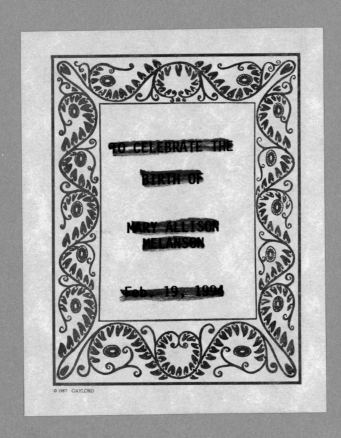

Lucy's Summer

WRITTEN BY

Donald Hall

ILLUSTRATED BY

Michael McCurdy

Browndeer Press
Harcourt Brace & Company
SAN DIEGO   NEW YORK   LONDON

Library of Congress Cataloging-in-Publication Data
Hall, Donald, 1928–
Lucy's summer/by Donald Hall; illustrated by
Michael McCurdy.
p.   cm.
"Browndeer Press."
Summary: For Lucy Wells, who lives on a farm in New Hampshire, the summer
of 1910 is filled with helping her mother can fruits and vegetables, enjoying
the Fourth of July celebration, and other activities.
ISBN 0–15–276873–4
[1. Summer — Fiction. 2. Farm life — New Hampshire — Fiction.
3. New Hampshire — Fiction.] I. McCurdy, Michael, ill. II. Title.
PZ7.H14115Lw   1995
[E] — dc20   93-17130

First edition   A B C D E

Printed in Singapore

The illustrations in this book were done in colored scratchboard on Rising Photolene paper.
The display type was set in Pabst Oldstyle.
The text type was set in Cloister by Thompson Type, San Diego, California.
Color separations were made by Bright Arts, Ltd., Singapore.
Printed and bound by Tien Wah Press, Singapore
This book was printed on Leykam recycled paper,
which contains more than 20 percent postconsumer waste and has a total
recycled content of at least 50 percent.
Production supervision by Warren Wallerstein and David Hough
Designed by Trina Stahl and Lori J. McThomas

Lucy Wells lived on a farm in New Hampshire with her mother Kate, her father Wesley, and her little sister Caroline.

The spring of 1910, when Lucy was seven, her mother turned the front parlor into a millinery shop, to sell hats to her neighbors in the backcountry.

Her mother wrote to Boston for fashion magazines and catalogs. She ordered supplies that came by Railway Express, and Lucy helped her unpack the boxes, and Caroline helped Lucy.

There were spools of silk and velvet ribbon.

There were swooping ostrich feathers and feathers from parrots as bright green as grass.

There were decorations that looked like real flowers and fruit.

"Look at *this!*" said Lucy, holding a bunch of plaster grapes that looked good enough to eat.

"Look at *this!*" said Caroline, sniffing a pink rose made out of velvet.

Ornaments hung in little wire baskets that dangled against the walls of the parlor where customers could see them, with the feathers in vases like flowers and rolls of ribbon on top of the fireplace mantel — blue, red, green, yellow, white, and purple.

The parlor looked like a flower shop or a tropical garden, full of exotic feathers and imported orchids.

Lucy's father painted MILLINERY above the front door.

Lucy's mother made a hat. She braided the foundation on a wire form and added ribbons and lace and feathers, and flowers and fruits.

"Look at *that!*" said Lucy and Caroline together.

Then Lucy's mother made another. And another. And another.

One rainy morning a carriage stopped outside the parlor, and Mrs. Hatcher, the wife of the blacksmith, tied her horse to the granite hitching post and came inside.

She bought a bright new hat with a yellow plume of feathers for summer and left an old hat to be fixed over for next winter.

Lucy's mother hugged Lucy and Caroline and gave each of them a penny.

Next Saturday her mother filled the wagon with hats, with Lucy and Caroline, and with a picnic lunch.

All day they drove over dirt lanes, back in the wooded hills.

So many houses Lucy had never seen before!

So many strange children who lived deep in the hills and went to tiny schools with only two or three others!

Lucy's mother sold six new hats.

She brought back three old hats to fix up over the summer and wrote directions in a little book: "Mrs. Hill — roses with blue lace." "Miss Jackson — green feathers and a green veil." "Mrs. Pemberton — grapes, cherries, violets, and daisies with red ribbon, but not too fancy."

On the way home they stopped near a stream and let Riley out of his shafts to graze and drink the water. Lucy and Caroline spread the picnic cloth on the grass under the tent of a willow tree that swept to the ground like a lady's skirt.

The picnic ended with custard pie.

By the end of June, Eagle Pond School closed for the summer. It was time for the summer's canning.

After the evening milking at four-thirty, and supper at five, Lucy's father and Anson, the hired man, carried baskets into the garden and brought back bushels of peas. Lucy, Caroline, and their mother sat in a row on the porch shelling peas into kettles until it got dark. The peas clattered into the bottom of the kettle like hail pounding on the roof.

Next morning, *all* morning until noon, Lucy's mother filled Ball jars with peas — ten quarts and twenty pints! — sweet and tender for next winter.

Then they lined up the jars on shelves in the dark root cellar.

Next week was strawberry time.

Lucy and Caroline picked over the berries and cut off the stems. Lucy ate fourteen, and Caroline eleven, and their fingers were stained bright red.

They made twenty-two jars of strawberry jam.

Next they canned rhubarb for winter pies.

On the Fourth of July the celebration in Danbury was the biggest of the year, with speeches and ice cream. The whole family stood on Main Street to watch the parade, with its matched horses and oxen, its floats from the 4–H Club, the Grange, and three different Sunday schools.

There were seven automobiles; Dr. Sleeper drove a Stanley Steamer.

A big clock that had been exhibited at the Chicago world's fair rode in a hayrack pulled by black horses.

Mrs. Hatcher, wearing Lucy's mother's hat, gave each of the girls a penny.

A speaker praised President Taft, and Lucy's father said, *"Hmph!"*

Some wild boys set off firecrackers, and a frightened horse reared and almost bolted. Mr. Millicent, the constable, gave the boys a talking to.

All through the summer Lucy and Caroline helped with canning — but when Lucy's mother washed or baked instead, the girls played house in a dark corner of the living room behind the cold stove.

"You fix the vegetables," Lucy said, pretending. "I'll put them up." She canned on her toy Glenwood range.

One day they canned a zillion pints.

Another day a man pulled into the yard in a closed wagon. He was a photographer with a big camera, and he offered to take the girls' pictures and develop them right then and there for only two dollars.

Lucy's mother used her hat money.

Lucy and Caroline dressed in their Sunday dresses, and Lucy put one arm around Caroline.

After one hour working in the back of his cart, the man delivered a beautiful, big photograph to Lucy's mother. Lucy thought it looked good of Caroline.

Some days the girls picked wildflowers in the woods, until once they saw a bear on the other side of the stream.

Another day a man walked along the road with a hand organ that he played and a monkey that begged for pennies with a silver cup. Lucy told Caroline that the monkey looked like Constable Millicent!

Their mother gave each of the girls a penny for the monkey.

Now all the women had their summer hats and wouldn't want their winter ones until the fall.

But one day Lucy heard a wagon stop in front, and someone came to the MILLINERY door.

Lucy peeked out the parlor window. She saw a gypsy caravan!

Almost every summer the gypsies came selling pots and pans. This time a woman knocked on the front door. A bedraggled hat hung over her pretty face, and she carried an armload of picture frames made of dark wood with carved wooden leaves at the corners.

Lucy knew: Her mother wanted a picture frame for their new photograph.

The woman looked hard at the hats. Lucy's mother looked hard at the frames.

The woman went back to the wagon wearing her new hat, and Lucy's mother had her picture frame, but soon they heard another knock on the front door.

The woman was back with her husband. He wanted decorations for *his* straw hat — cherries? or maybe a feather?

Lucy's mother put a striped ribbon around his hat, and bright cherries, and a white feather. Now she had two picture frames.

In August it didn't rain for weeks, and the vegetables looked weary and the hay turned brown.

Then one hot night there was a terrible thunderstorm.

Lucy and Caroline hugged each other in bed as lightning flashed around them. "Last year in Danbury lightning hit the Lebeaus' barn and burned it down!" Lucy whispered to Caroline. Both girls shivered.

The next morning they saw that hail stones — they must have been as big as pullets' eggs! — had knocked down hay and daylilies and tomatoes.

Then they canned one hundred Ball jars of pickled beets.

They canned two hundred quarts of string beans, snapping them on the porch after supper.

They canned a hundred pints of corn niblets and two hundred quarts of tomatoes.

They made a green tomato relish called piccalilli.

The root cellar filled with wonderful things to eat all winter long. Lucy was proud when she looked at the rows of jars. She could tell that her mother was proud, too.

"We'll be glad next winter," Lucy told Caroline.

Once at night as they sat around the oil lamp, Lucy looked up from her book and laughed out loud.

"Everyone cans things to eat!" she said. "Momma cans all day for us. Bees can honey. Squirrels can acorns. When Poppa stacks hay in the barn, he cans for the cows!"

Then it was the first of September. Lucy helped dust the parlor and shine the mirror to be ready for the fall hat season.

One evening the whole family sat around the table in the living room under the bright oil lamp as Lucy's mother finished remaking last year's winter hats the way people had asked her to — "roses with blue lace"; "green feathers and a green veil"; "grapes, cherries, violets, and daisies with red ribbon."

Suddenly Lucy's mother said, "It won't do. I need material for winter hats, and I need to see the new fashions. Wesley, I need to go to Boston."

Boston was only three hours away by train, but practically nobody saw any reason to go there.

Lucy asked, "Can I come, too?"

Her mother looked surprised. "Certainly," she said.

Lucy was excited. No one from Eagle Pond School had ever been to Boston!

Lucy packed her six pennies, and they took the "Peanut" from Gale at seven o'clock — past farms and mill towns all the way to Boston's North Station.

Boston's sidewalks were crowded with more people than Lucy had seen in her whole life.

Buildings bigger than barns — five times bigger! — rose into the smoky air, along the seven blocks to the wholesale millinery district.

For lunch they went to a sidewalk restaurant, where they ate sitting outside,

looking at millions of people hurrying past them on the street.

    Lucy ate oyster stew for the first time in her life, while her mother had frankfurts with Boston baked beans.

    For dessert they both had red Jell-O with whipped cream.

    In one big store Lucy's mother bought seven spools of the brightest ribbon.

    In another she bought yards of velvet in dark colors to make linings for winter hats.

    In another she bought feathers and beads.

    In another she bought cloth flowers and plaster fruits.

After lunch they had an hour before the afternoon Peanut left North Station.

"Come with me," said Lucy's mother. "There's something I want to show you."

Lucy followed her mother through the aisles of a huge Woolworth's until they came to a long, long counter — "as long as a *hayrack,*" Lucy told Caroline before they went to sleep that night — which was filled, from one end to the other, with toys that cost one penny each!

There were tiny china dolls, so beautiful, about one inch long, with black hair and little red circles painted on white cheeks. One penny each.

There were tiny kettles and skillets, just the right size for Lucy's toy Glenwood range at home. One penny each.

There were sets of tiny cups and saucers, dolls' tea sets. One penny for a cup and saucer.

Best, there were tiny dolls' hot water bottles with rubber stoppers that fit. One penny each.

When the Peanut pulled into Gale that evening, Lucy's father and Caroline were waiting with Riley, and on the way back to the farm Caroline squeezed her new doll and her tiny hot water bottle.

Lucy told Caroline about Boston, oyster stew, and the long, long counter at Woolworth's. She cooked with her toy skillet on her toy Glenwood.

That night around the lamp, Lucy and Caroline made tiny hats for their tiny, new china dolls.

The next morning Lucy held Caroline's hand and took her to her first day at Eagle Pond School.

They brought their new dolls with them, with their tiny hats, and in their lunch bags they carried a sandwich and a slice of pie — made from the rhubarb they had canned long ago in June.

AFTERWORD

A LONG TIME AGO, my mother Lucy and her sister Caroline lived in a New Hampshire farmhouse with their father and mother, who milked cows and raised sheep. As I grew up, my mother told me stories of her childhood — about her mother's millinery shop, about a long counter of penny toys at Woolworth's, and about a doll's hot water bottle.

Now ninety years old, my mother has left her Connecticut house and come north to a nursing facility near us in New Hampshire. My wife and I, who live in the farmhouse where my mother was born, see her every day, and often we reminisce about the past. Upstairs in the back chamber, where everything comes to rest — a tiny china doll, a doll-size kettle — we still find the old hat pedestals upon which my grandmother displayed her millinery, their dusky stems rising like iron crabgrass under the eaves.

—D. H.